≠
E
F534a

THE ABC EXHIBIT

▼ ▼ ▼

ABCD
EFGHI
JKLM
NOPQR
STU
XYZW

THE ABC EXHIBIT

LEONARD EVERETT FISHER

▼ ▼ ▼

MACMILLAN PUBLISHING COMPANY   NEW YORK

Collier Macmillan Canada   Toronto

Maxwell Macmillan International Publishing Group

New York   Oxford   Singapore   Sydney

▼ ▼ ▼

Macmillan Publishing Company
866 Third Avenue, New York, NY 10022
Collier Macmillan Canada, Inc.
1200 Eglinton Avenue East, Suite 200
Don Mills, Ontario M3C 3N1
First edition   Printed in the United States of America

1   2   3   4   5   6   7   8   9   10

Library of Congress Cataloging-in-Publication Data
Fisher, Leonard Everett.
The ABC exhibit/Leonard Everett Fisher.
—1st ed.   p.   cm.
Summary: Introduces the letters of the alphabet in
paintings of subjects from Acrobat to Zinnia.
I S B N 0 - 0 2 - 7 3 5 2 5 1 - X
1. English language—Alphabet—Juvenile literature.
[1. Alphabet.] I. Title.
PE1155.F56   1991   [E]—dc20
90-6639   CIP   AC

For

Beverly **R**eingold

Judith **R. W**hipple

Cecilia **Y**ung

▼ ▼ ▼

Acrobat

Balloon

▼ ▼ ▼

C l o u d

▼ ▼ ▼

Duck

▼ ▼ ▼

Elephant

▼ ▼ ▼

Fog

▼ ▼ ▼

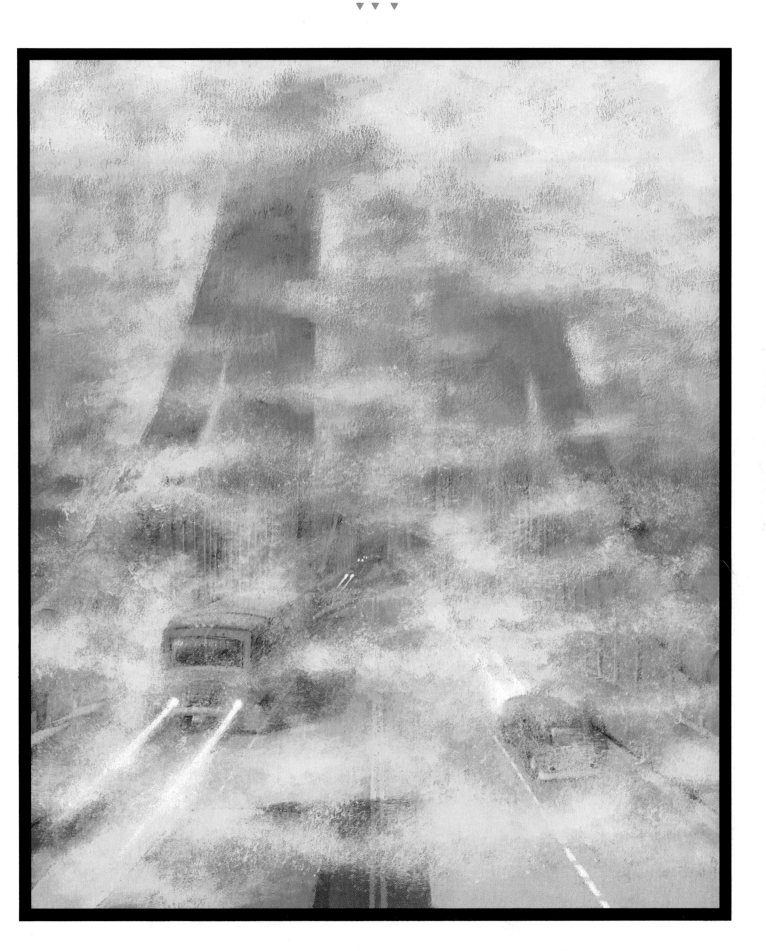

Guitar

Hat

▼ ▼ ▼

Iceberg

▼ ▼ ▼

Juggler

Kite

▼ ▼ ▼

Lightning

Mountain

▼ ▼ ▼

Nest

Orange

▼ ▼ ▼

Parrot

▼ ▼ ▼

Quartet

▼ ▼ ▼

Ribbon

▼ ▼ ▼

Sailboat

▼ ▼ ▼

Target

▼ ▼ ▼

Umbrella

▾ ▾ ▾

Veil

▼ ▼ ▼

Wall

▼ ▼ ▼

Xylophone
▼ ▼ ▼

Yo-yo

▼ ▼ ▼

Zinnia

Leonard Everett Fisher prepared the artwork

for this book in acrylics on board.

The text was set by Cardinal Type Service, Inc., in Baker Signet Bold,

with initial caps in Baker Signet Bold Extended.

The artwork was color separated by VCM Graphics, Inc.,

and the book was printed by United Lithographing Corporation

on 80 pound Patina Matte paper.

It was bound by The Book Press, Inc.

▼ ▼ ▼